The Snowy Day

It is a snowy day.
There is a lot to do.

What does Happy do?
Happy makes a snowman.

What does the bird do?
The bird makes a friend.

What does Grumpy do?
Grumpy makes a face.

What does the Prince do?
The Prince makes a fire.

What does Snow White do?
Snow White makes soup.

It is a snowy day.
Let's eat!